Crossfire Southwest

life behind a badge

stories by **Michael A. DeMarco**, M.A.

Printed in the United States of America

The paper in this book meets the guidelines for permanence and durability of the Committee on Production Guidelines for Book Longevity of the Council on Library Resources.

Copyright © 2024
Via Media Publishing Company
941 Calle Mejia #822, Santa Fe, NM 87501 USA
E-mail: contact@viamediapublishing.com

Cover design by Via Media Publishing Company.
Abstract watercolor sketch of police officer.
ID 179786392 © Nathings /Dreamstime.com
Watercolor desert landscape with cactuses and mountains.
ID 203216797 © rotorania | www.123rf.com
Vintage bronze police badge with star.
ID Vintage bronze Police badge with star © natbasil | www.123rf.com

ISBN 979-8-218-39559-9

www.viamediapublishing.com

Dedication

Gratitude to all law enforcement officers

who oftentimes serve under precarious conditions

and immense distress, and whose compassionate devotion

to the public shines unflinchingly through their daily work.

A special thanks to those who have shared

information about their work for this book.

Contents

Red or Green?

The waitress waddles over to our table in her black stretch pants that only serve to accentuate a bulging midriff. She knows I usually order *huevos rancheros* . . . the traditional egg dish for ranchers. Managing to bat her extra long eyelashes, crusted with liner, she asks: "Red or green?"

Geez, I can't decide now. The color of chile seems insignificant. I'm so anxious. We've come here to talk of much more important matters. Tessie, my fiance for the last two years of college, looks sympathetically at me with her warm ebony eyes, and says, "Braden, let's just enjoy a drink and chat for awhile. We're in no hurry. We can select breakfast later."

Her words flow out like honey. Her compassion and placid demeanor calms me, turning my fretting frown into a smile. Tessie orders a coffee for herself and, for me, an iced tea.

"Okay Braden, you've obviously been troubled these past few weeks since graduation. It's not like you to keep your thoughts inside, hidden from me. Since I've known you these past four years, I have never seen you like this. My handsome man—at 6 foot 4, you are as sensitive as you are tall. Tell me what's on your mind. Let's talk about whatever is bothering you."

I'm a lucky man to have met this woman. It's a miracle how things happen, how fate introduced us. Tessie is the central figure around which all my other thoughts are circling. We start to reminisce of the early days meeting on campus in the fall of 1968, four years ago. Our friendship progressed slowly but steadily over the months. I open up and reaffirm how she holds the most special place in my heart. Love crept up from behind and engulfed us. Seems this is now my dilemma.

I go on explaining to Tessie that I, Braden Vicentin, am an East Coast guy with Irish-Italian roots who came to the Southwest to continue my education, not knowing I'd fall in love with a very traditional Hispanic girl. I didn't need a passport to get here—as some believe is necessary—but I landed in a foreign place nonetheless. Because I had a hard time in high school, my father thought it best I go to a small Catholic school as not to be submerged by a massive student enrollment at a large university, such as Boston College.

My dad's criteria greatly limited my choice to only two options. Solely on gut feeling, I chose to go to Aldea Baca College in the city of Aldea Baca, Arizona. It's about a five hour drive from here to the Mexico border. The old town is well-known for its deep historical blend of Spanish and Native American cultures. This is the furthest of the two colleges from my hometown in North Carolina.

When I first arrived at the train station that's eighteen miles from Aldea Baca, I was seventeen years old. Three people got off the train, including myself. Like a scene in an old Western movie, we found ourselves in the middle of a sun-baked desert, cactus country, nearly devoid of signs of civilization. There was one van waiting to take us out of the one street, one restaurant town, to the relatively bustling city of Aldea Baca. I remember blurting out: "Oh bejesus! Did I make the biggest mistake in my life coming here?"

The people here in Arizona are different! Clothing, food, climate, language, art… and much you can't actually see or feel. It's a place with an alternate vision of the world. History. Attitudes. Customs. I've adapted some to living here in Aldea Baca, but the small city often seems overwhelming. I've been somewhat sheltered on campus much of the time and in the company of other gringos and understanding locals who put up with our awkward attempts to fit in.

Tessie accepts me fully. Why she does, I may never know. I guess she's able to look past all the superficial stuff. She's an old soul with penetrating vision, accurate intuition, and a quick, dry wit. Even before we started dating, she was helpful while I was recovering from a serious injury from a head-on collision that happened while trying to run a pig skin into the end zone. She also helped me greatly with my struggles with recently diagnosed dyslexia. Many thought I was just mentally unable to do well academically—their kind way of saying I'm a dummy. Even my father has his doubts, but he always encourages me.

It took a year for my head injury to fully heal and the dyslexia eventually became manageable. I battled through the therapy sessions with a reading specialist, making good progress. Being dyslexic actually helped me in unexpected ways, such as memorization. Since I have a difficult time reading and writing, I simply memorize material for school and daily life. My brain acts like duct tape, effortlessly holding on to facts and figures. Even with things I'd rather forget about!

Tessie helped even while I was dating Charmaine, a French foreign student on campus at that time. We met when I arrived on campus for my first semester. The mademoiselle was a great gal too. She may have shown me the world, but we amicably parted ways when she returned to France. Tessie and Charmaine were friends. Tessie continued to be in my circle of friends. Over the following months our friendship slowly grew closer and closer as if destined. Now we face the future together, come what may.

My parents know we are dating and no doubt think it's temporary and I'd return to the East Coast soon after graduation. Dad is open minded and only wants me to be happy. If that means someday I'll marry Tessie, that'd be fine with him. In the opposite corner, my mom can't understand why I would even think to date a girl of a "different race." Lordy. I've tried to explain to her that Tessie isn't of a different race, but failed to get through her thick wall of bias. Mom persistently reminds me that a highschool sweetheart is still available and waiting for my return east.

Then there are Tessie's relatives. All know she is dating an outsider. They don't say much to her about it, probably just wishing the relationship would fizzle and I'd depart. But, our relationship has only gotten stronger. During the recent Christmas holiday, I chose not to go to my parents and remained here to be with Tessie. Her family prepared for a grand fiesta as usual. When Tessie mentioned that I'd be here, there was objection among the elders. I was not to be invited. Tessie chose to spend the holiday celebrating with me, just the two of the few on campus, rather than intrude in the house with all her relatives.

I had some insecurities while dating Tessie. She had her friendly charm. Any time we were out in town, she'd be met by a number of young men who were always thrilled to see her. My guess was that, when they saw my intimidating size, they were careful to not be outwardly flirtatious with her.

"Braden, this is my cousin Eduardo." "Braden, this is my cousin George." "Cousin Luis, this is Braden."

I just didn't feel Tessie could have so many male cousins. Turns out, she does! Over time, I somehow managed to construct a large ancestral chart in my head to comprehend her complex family relationships. While figuring out the *gran familia*, I also learned just how dedicated she was to our relationship.

I sum up with Tessie the thoughts and feelings I have about our families, explaining how I worry that they may somehow break us apart. She sits quietly listening, chin resting on her palm, elbow on the table. I didn't add anything to what she already knew, but I just vocalized my sentiments.

"Ahh Braden," she sighs, "I've thought about the negative clouds that some of our relatives try to bring over our heads. Remember, most are fine with us being together. Only a few object, but we don't need to worry about them. As the family matron, my grandmother is only trying to preserve our family traditions. She'll eventually be swayed by your charming ways! Your mom is certainly the strongest one opposed to us being together. The few times I've met her, I expected her to chase me away swinging a shillelagh! Maybe it's a good thing she lives over two-thousand miles away."

I cut in here with deep sympathy for my mom. I know and understand her ways. Luckily I've learned from my dad how to deal with her.

"Well, I can just ignore her. Can you?"

"Yes, Braden. She has her own dream for you, but we have ours. Let's not worry about the relatives. What is really important is our own relationship, you and I, this is all that matters to me. I'm happy with us. I don't worry about the others. We'll be fine. Don't you think?"

"I feel much better knowing you feel this way. I want to fit in with your family and would like them to be at ease in my presence."

"Do you have other concerns dear Braden? Does

anything about me bother you? My lifestyle here?

"Oh no, no, no . . . You do come down hard on me sometimes, but it seems only when I deserve it, which is often enough. I'm actually happy about that. You've helped me improve my ways of thinking here, especially about cultural differences. I'm totally content with how we are together. I guess I'm just wondering about our families' being comfortable with us, and other things . . . like where to live, where to work, and how to be financially stable."

"All those types of things will fall into place Braden. We've just graduated from college. It will take time."

We continue talking about my concerns. I have to move out of the dormitory soon. Tessie knows of some apartments to consider. She also knows many people in town who could help. Father Tito from Saint Anne's Church may know some families who rent out space.

Just last week I did receive a nice job offer in Chicago at a financial institute. The offered starting salary is quite good. I tell Tessie about this, although I really don't want to go to Chicago. We refocus on my staying here.

"Braden, that is only your first job offer. There will be other offers. You haven't started looking in this area yet. We have time. We can look for an apartment for you and also job hunt. For now, I have my part-time bookkeeping work at the state educational department. Plus, because I'm living at my mom's home, without any big obligation, I have free time to help you. If you really want to live here so we can be together, without worrying about what family members think—we really only need to find you work and a place to live."

"Your right Tessie. You know, when I think of you, all else doesn't really matter. All those questions I had in my mind when we arrived at the restaurant—the worry about families, finances, work, and all—actually are not so important. So, it comes down to only two things: finding a place to stay and a place to work."

"Great, Braden! This coming Monday we can plan on diving into the job search. For now, I'm hungry!"

Tessie flags down the waitress and orders a breakfast burrito. After I predictably order the *huevos rancheros*, out comes the question from our waitress: "Red or green, señor?"

Now my decision in easy to make.

"Christmas"—both red and green together. The mix will bring zest to the dish.

Never Fired a Gun

Scoping out potential employers located within fifty miles of Tessie's home, together we develop a list. Unless I'd like to be a waiter, the list is short. Being a college graduate makes my resume strong, excelling in mathematics. I hand-deliver applications to a half-dozen places. Three weeks later I get invited for an interview at the Lincoln Savings and Loan on Mission Street. They feel they have a perfect position for me. I tell them that I'd think about it and get back to them in a day or two. Eager to start work—any kind of work—I accepted the next day, which was a Wednesday. The manager tells me to start work on Monday. I have to arrive on time, wearing a tie.

The office building atmosphere is fine, but it only took a few weeks for me to realize that the new job is pure torture. Boring paperwork is turning me into a zombie. The topic of work comes up while Tessie and I are at a Thanksgiving gathering with former classmates. While I chat with a friend who is also from the east coast, Tessie is nearby speaking in Spanish with three classmates. Turns out all three had recently joined the Aldea Baca Police Department.

Tessie calls me over. "Braden, you remember these guys who were in a few of our classes?"

I half expected Tessie to say these chaps are cousins, but then recognize their familiar faces. Their girlfriends are longtime friends of Tessie.

"Yes, hello guys. I haven't seen any of you since graduation night."

Tessie enlivens the conversation by joking about their girlfriends, then gradually brings in the topic of finding work in the city. One in the group responds to her prodding and tells me of their new work.

"The police department is hiring. Most working there finished high school, but didn't go on to college. They usually spent a few years in the military instead. So now the department is paying bonuses for college-educated people to join. If you get hired, you'd be given a uniform and training. Just go to their office and they'll give you all the details."

A grin appears on his face when he adds, "I'm sure they could use a big macho man like you to patrol the bars!"

After the chuckle, I turn to Tessie to talk seriously about this prospect. I can't really decide on anything of importance without consulting her, even though we're not engaged yet. The two times I did ask her to marry me, she turned me down, saying she wanted to get an advanced university degree before getting hitched. I think there's still a chance, so I keep treating her as if wedding bells will eventually sound. This is a big part of why I'm seeking work here, even if it means becoming a cop. The job has its risks. I have a fairly good idea of what being a policeman would entail, because my father is an FBI agent and such work often came into our conversations since my childhood. Despite the potential dangers associated with the work, Tessie didn't object to my joining the police force.

On Monday morning I call the personnel department and ask if they have any openings and about the application process. A lady says, if I'm serious about applying, it's best to come in person to discuss all the details. So I drive fifteen minutes to the station and I speak to a front desk person, who speaks to somebody else, who speaks to somebody else, and eventually I get word: "Just wait here. The chief wants to talk to you. While you wait, you can fill out these papers—our exam is part of the application process."

Answering the test questions seems easy enough. Sitting on a hardwood chair, waiting to meet the chief, is what seems like an eternity.

I finally get called in for the interview. I don't know who the chief of police is from anyone else wearing a uniform. I get led through a large room with about eight officers chatting in Spanish, and pass through a doorway to enter the chief's office. Two men introduce themselves as an assistant chief and a captain. The guy planted at a big desk behind them must be Chief Sam Rivera, as stamped on the nameplate in front of a phone and stacks of papers. He's a stocky ex-Marine with twenty-five years on the force and ten as chief. He said that he'll interview me for the job and asks the other two men to leave.

Chief Rivera shoots a few questions at me in machine gun fashion, zeroing in on personal matters. He wants to know about me and my family background.

"I'm not from here," as if he didn't intuit that fact immediately upon first glance. "I'm from North Carolina. I went to college here and I want to get a job here."

The chief is impressed with my father's work in the FBI, and less so that I've never fired a gun before in my life. He must be thinking, "This young man is tall and formidable looking. Perhaps he's trainable."

After he extracts a few more details about me, my parents and brothers, he turns the focus on my list of references. He sits up straight, noticing Tessie's name and a few of her relatives. With a raised eyebrow, he begins to speak softly.

"*Familia de Ortiz* . . . Her family lives in Tierra Redonda? They have relatives further south, near the Coconino National Forest area?"

"Yes," I said, "she lives with her mother and grandfather in Tierra Redonda and her an uncle Ricky lives just up the main road. I've been out there are a number of times over the years, but I've spent most of my time at the dormitories and now I have an apartment here in town."

Twiddling with his thick mustache, the chief's mind drifts off for extra-long seconds. Like reading writing on a wall, I see by his manner that he instinctively realizes that Tessie is my girlfriend. It turns out that the chief knows her family very well. Smiling, he starts to rattle on about Tessie's family members by their first names. Speaking on the edge of his seat, he becomes more and more animated with each story. He slowly calms and leans back into his leather-padded chair. Then he leans forward as if he's about the confess some secret, saying in a heavy Hispanic accent, "Well… ya know… *estas personas…* these people are pretty good people—*muy buena gente.*"

"Yes, yes. They certainly are," nodding my head in near total agreement while wondering how the hell does this guy knows all the Ortiz family so well.

He picks up the phone and calls Anna Perez, head of personnel, saying to her: "He's hired. He starts today."

He tells me to be back at four o'clock at the council chambers in the other wing in the same building to go through steps to be formally hired. When I arrive, Commander Greg Garcia is running the show. He's a bulldog, biting into me roughly for absolutely no reason. He just doesn't seem to like me.

"You need a haircut by tomorrow. I'm assigning you a training officer, Richard Lopez, who will take you under his wing for the next three months."

Something slows his thought process and he asks, "Vicentin? . . . Any relation to an agent who taught at FBI Quantico?"

"That would be my father, Sir."

From that moment onward, Commander Garcia's

disposition changed. He had studied at Quantico a decade ago. My father was one of his instructors. The commander now starts treating me like royalty. Seems fresh air entered the room. We sign papers and Commander Greg Garcia welcomes me as an official member of the force with a vigorous handshake.

I get introduced to Richard Lopez, my training officer, who brings news that they are short one officer for the graveyard shift. Out of the whirlwind's hiring process, I'm stunned to hear: "Your assignment is it to patrol the downtown in a squad car. You'll need to get your gear before starting your shift."

Lopez leads me to the basement where another officer helps me pick out clothing for a novice policeman. Thoughts silently surface in my head that a uniform will make me look admirable and reflect my new authoritative position. I hope the gallant image will impress Tessie and her family too. I smile proudly with these fanciful thoughts.

Turns out that the average height of men on the force is under five foot ten. I tower almost a foot above them. As a result, I'm given pants with the longest length available. They are about three inches short. The cuffs on a new blue shirt aren't close to reaching my wrists. The hat's tight. As the officer hands a holster to me, I say "It's on the wrong side."

He's puzzled and asks, "How can it be on the wrong side?"

"I'm left-handed. Shouldn't the holster be on my left side?"

"Ohhh," he muffles out under his breath, then adds, "You'll have to learn to shoot right-handed."

To top it all off, he hands me a Colt revolver that obviously has a slightly bent barrel. I actually start silently contemplating if the pistol could be useful for shooting around corners…

As I stand in full dress in front of a mirror, I can't fully believe what I see! The dignified image of me in uniform that I had created earlier today has mutated into an embarrassing comic figure, an image I'll need to bear as a rookie for the coming months, or perhaps years.

Now I'm dressed with someplace to go and something to do. Just exactly where to do what, I'm not sure. I ask Officer Lopez for guidance.

"You get in the car and slowly cruise around the streets. Return the car at the end of your shift."

Thus on the chilly night of October 1, 1972, begins my working for the Aldea Baca Police Department.

Bathroom Cleanup

As a relatively new officer, I am to attend a briefing every day as required by our shift commander. The briefing room is a twenty-by-thirty foot area with a few rows of chairs. It is here that officers receive instructions, paychecks, assignments for the day, general orders and specific orders, and announcements. Behind the back of this room is a small restroom, about six-by-eight foot with a toilet, a urinal, and a sink.

After one of the briefings, some officers leave to get out on their patrols or to desk duties. A few remain discussing the topics of the day. Two of the men, Teddy and Jaime, get into a heated disagreement, and one of them walks away while the other is in mid-sentence. While the first heads into the restroom, the other follows in right behind him. We could hear the argument inside working up to a vocal crescendo. Soon follow multiple rounds of gunfire! All of a sudden the gunfire stops.

All of us understand that the room is only about eight feet long by about six feet wide, and can't imagine the results of the flying lead. Officers turn their focus on me. I notice even the sergeant's eyes are glued my way. I guess because I'm the newest officer on the force, he says "Go in and find out what happened."

Under order, I have no choice but to open the door and enter the restroom. I see the two men, Teddy and Jaime, in frozen stances with smoking guns in their hands. They are white as ghosts. Water is coming out of the sink and out of the toilet. The paper towel dispenser, which was on the opposite side of the room, is now on the ground. Gun smoke swirls through the air filling our nostrils with its aroma. By the sound of the shooting, it seems they had fired every bullet from their chambers. All I could say to the two officers is "Put your guns in your holsters."

When I point the way back into the briefing room, the sergeant takes the officers' guns, opens them up, and looks into the cylinders. He looks at me saying, "They shot them all—each twelve rounds out of both revolvers and they come out of the toilet without scratches. Two experienced officers, standing less than eight feet apart, shoot six rounds at each other, managing to miss their targets." His last sentence fades, but his head continues shaking in disbelief.

Sarge asks me what the room looks like.

I tell him, "The boys shot out the faucet, so a geyser is spouting out above the sink. The toilet has chunks of ceramic missing and is flooding over. The ceramic sink is cracked too. Seems flying debris knocked big chunks out of the adobe walls. A bullet flew out the window on the back wall."

The sergeant says, "I think you need to book them."

"I may be the low man on the totem pole here," I say with some hesitation, "but I'm not booking anyone. This is an internal problem. Since I'm not certified, I could go to jail for making an arrest. Seems best if you

do it, sir, since you have the most authority among us."

Sarge talks to himself: "Shooting six times . . . Who can miss anything at that close range? They need to go back to the firing range."

No Parking Zone

Routine days on the police beat are never routine. This is what I'm learning as the weeks turn to months facing each new day. I'm still working night shifts. Guess I'll be considered a rookie for the next few years. When I and others attend tonight's briefing, we learn that the city is calm, usual for a mid-week night.

The main piece of news we receive deals with a problem suitable for the city maintenance crew. Atop a small hill overlooking the city there's an area with a flooding problem. The cause of the flooding is unknown at this time. Perhaps it was caused by a minor accident? Perhaps there's an underground stream or a waterline burst? Since the location offers great views that extend over the city and miles of desert, locals like to go there day or evening times. We're told there's a giant pool of water there and the ground is not stable. Presenting some danger for cars, half the area has been marked off with yellow tape. Hopefully nobody will try to drive into this zone. We are told to check this area while driving on our patrol to make sure everything is okay.

A few hours go by as we patrol city streets, eyeing areas for any problems to tend to.

About 1:45am, a call comes into the main office.

"Unit 15 calling in. . . . I'm sinking."

Dispatcher responds: "What? Please repeat."

"Unit 15. I'm sinking!"

"Sinking? What? Sinking?" asks the dispatcher

in a voice of disbelief. "Where are you 15?"

"I'm in a big pit. I got into a big pit and I'm sinking with water and mud around the car."

Yes, unit 15 is stuck on the overlook. My brain calculates that perhaps he pulled over to snooze. Since I'm in a car with a partner in the area, the dispatcher radios for us to go to the overlook to search for unit 15. When we turn into to parking area, we see Luke, our brother in blue, sitting on top of his car. The car has sunk far enough that the wheel wells are not visible. Luke had crawled out his side window to get out of the car and onto the roof top.

My partner, Joe Fernandez, gets out of our car and starts to walk toward Luke's car. At a distance, he yells at Luke, "Listen! I'm not gonna get my uniform dirty trying to get you out of this mud pit!"

I make a suggestion. "Hey Joe, let's call for a wrecker to tow him out."

About thirty minutes later, the truck arrives. The driver, Jake, doesn't hesitate to wade hip-deep in water to hook up Luke's vehicle. Water is now nearing the roof of the car as Jake pulls the wrecker ahead far enough for the chains to become taught. Very slowly, the truck budges the car inch by inch forward with Luke screaming. I don't know why a grown man would scream in this case. Odds are that Luke doesn't know how to swim.

With a good deal of wheel spinning, mud flying,

and cussing, the wrecker pulls forward. Unit 15, with Señor Luke sitting front and center on top of the car, is now out of the mud pit and onto terra firma. This is only one of many rare occurrences that spice up a night shift routine.

Aldea Baca's Annual Festival

For our city, Aldea Baca's annual festival is always the grandest gathering of the year in celebration of the city's history and culture. Just about everyone living in the city participates as well as a flood of people coming in from the surrounding area. It's a busy time for the police department.

The main intersections into the city center are patrolled. Police officers man four entrances and exits through the plaza area. Three or four officers' only duty is to stay at those barricades. We must be able to move the barricades in case emergency vehicles need to enter the downtown.

Since I've only been on the force for less than a year, this is the first time I'm assigned to this duty. I'm playing sentinel along with two other officers at the corner in front of a historic hotel. We're particularly fussy to keep the way clear for emergency vehicles. Parking spaces have been taken since early morning. There will be much car traffic all day, mainly driving in circles. With luck, they may find some parking space a few blocks away.

I'm standing on the sidewalk catty corner to the hotel. A stream of bikers roar onto the pavement and the lead biker rolls up to me.

"Hey officer, we want to go into the hotel. Can we park our bikes here?"

Faces of about a dozen men and their ladies stare

at me. I have sympathy for them and make a deal.

"You can parallel park, with bikes facing the street in case there's a need to move them quickly. A couple bikers must stay with the bikes. If there is any problem, they can notify you to move the bikes."

The man removes a black leather glove and shakes my hand. "Deal." They all park in an organized, well mannered fashion.

For the next few hours, I stroll around the wooden barricade guiding cars and greeting visitors who are enjoying the festival foods and activities.

Later in the afternoon, a hotel employee rushes up to me. Some patrons are slugging it out at the bar. I get in the squad car to radio in with details. Two officers will remain at the barricade and I'll go into the hotel bar to investigate.

I hastily walk across the street along with the hotel employee and we enter the bar. A group of bikers have broken a few chairs. Some of their foes are knocked out laying on the floor. Others ran out the door to safety. Remaining in the room is a burley group of roughneck biker types. They're standing, staring at me like coyotes staring at fresh meat. They look ready to attack, but then just freeze in their tracks. Why they didn't take a single step toward me was puzzling. I was certainly outnumbered.

The alpha guys in front of the group have roving eyes. I notice they are looking behind me. I turn and see a wall of men standing at my back and recognize their leader. He's the guy I had talked with earlier about parking the bikes. A couple of his guys heard the conversation between me and the agitators and decided to back me up, if needed.

I tell the leader, "I know they're afraid of you, but I think there will be no need to jump in. All looks resolved here. Thanks for your support. It turned the heat down for sure."

Then I turn to the head of the other biker group, giving him a short lecture. They pony up a bunch of money to the hotel to cover the damages and leave. This was a highpoint during the day's drinking. In part, the annual festival is defined by the drinking activities inside bars as well as outside on the streets.

Faceoff with Goliath

When I became a line officer, I was assigned to attend a bar for a Friday night scuffle. The police handbook defines a line officer as one who is skilled for handling situations such as problem-solving and conflict resolution. It requires some quick, on the spot decision-making. A good number of Arizona bars claim fame for being rough places where fights often break out.

I get orders to get to Bar Herradura on Washington Avenue as soon as possible. Fight in progress. By time I do arrive, the fight is over but a number of people have obviously been injured. Outside the front door, some are holding bloody wounds. Some are lying on the ground. Just from the sight outside, I feel it best to radio the sergeant for backup.

He responds, saying "Officer Vicentin, you have one fight scene. We'll send one officer. You."

I'm on my own and decide to go into the bar, not knowing what to expect. The place is trashed. Tables broken. Behind the long wooden bar, glasses and most of the liquor bottles are broken. Seems a dozen large dust devils stormed through the place.

Who do I see remaining inside the Herradura? One giant of a man is sitting at the end of the bar by himself. The biggest man I've ever seen. Off to the side, a good distance from Goliath, are a lot of people in pain, sitting down, holding their aching heads or arms.

I walk up behind the man, who's staring ahead at

the wall's broken mirror.

"Hey champ, can I help you?"

This guy turns around and starts to stand up. I am six foot two inches tall and weigh about 220 pounds. He turns toward me and stands up. He seems close to a foot taller than I am. My shadow would easily fit inside his. I tell him that he needs to tell me about what happened.

He snarls out that "A little pipsqueak was making fun of me, so I decided to teach him lesson."

While gazing over the room, I say, "It looks like you've taught everybody else a lesson too."

He agrees, explaining that he knew he shouldn't have done what he did. Now it registers that he's in trouble with the law.

"You know I have to arrest you and I'm required to put handcuffs on you.

He is watching me like I'm a ladybug, and I'm wondering if this will be my last Friday ever, not just in a bar. Will he pound me into the ground?

He didn't contort his face in anticipation for any attack. He just tells me, "Officer, you're not gonna be able to get those on me."

I get a little bit more forceful, saying "I have to put these on you. It's okay. Let me have your hands."

He starts raising his hands to his front, so I say "Behind your back."

I cuff his left wrist and quickly realize that it is impossible to cuff his other wrist. The handcuffs are about two inches too short. I would need to connect two sets of handcuffs to span to the job.

"Well, you're right. It doesn't look like I can handcuff you, but you're gonna have to get into the car so we can go to the station."

When we get outside, he looks at the police car, then looks at me like I'm joking. He doesn't think he can get into the car. I'm wondering if the law of physics will prevent it. I tell him to try, which he did for about ten minutes. He was working up a sweat. He couldn't get in. He is just too gigantic to get into a normal sized car. He drives a truck. There is only one option. I share my idea.

"Well, you know the police station is just a couple blocks away. We can walk."

When we get within thirty feet from the station entrance, the front doors swing open and the sergeant is rushing out to the sidewalk. He immediately notices two big lugs approaching and becomes apprehensive. His eyes adjust to the dark and he recognizes me. He says he was just heading to the bar, worried because I haven't answered the radio for a while.

"Sarge, I had to walk him here. I couldn't handcuff him and he doesn't fit in my car."

We go into the station. Sarge tells me to book the giant and returns to his desk. I book Goliath upstairs in the jail. I figured he would be released on his own recognizance after he posts a $25 bond, so I don't even bother putting the gargantuan hombre in a cell.

Friendly Fire and Ice

Winter is pleasant here and especially welcomed following a blistering hot summer. We rarely get even a dusting of snow, but when it does snow, aromas rise from the desert that invigorate one's whole being. If flakes do fall, it is usually during the night when the lowest temperatures of the day occur.

Tonight is just such a frosted night when we get a midnight dispatch for two officers to go to Freeman Cemetery. Tombstones here date to the early 1800s when it was established as a private cemetery for the prominent people in the area. Later, as family members died out or moved away, the amount of money that was collected every year for the cemetery's upkeep starting to dwindle. As a result, the remaining heirs decided to legally turn it over to the City of Aldea Baca, primarily as a potter's field—a place for the burial of unknown, unclaimed or impoverished people. What could be going on here on this magical snowy night?

Today there is a pretty good amount of snow on Freeman's frozen ground. At the entrance gate, we turn on our flashlights and get out of the patrol car. The flashlight allows me to see about two-hundred feet. Along the ground I can see footprints leading to an old marble mausoleum, the largest in the cemetery. I walk a distance to the right not to disturb the prints in the snow. We may need to make a cast of them later. Pete, my partner, is walking on the left of the tracks. No prints lead away from the mausoleum. Pete is about one-hundred feet to the mausoleum and I'm behind him about twenty feet holding a steady light beam towards the distinctive bronze doors.

Pete motions that he sees some movement in the mausoleum. This probably isn't a simple intrusion to damage property, but perhaps this is an attempt to rob the grave. Getting apprehensive, Pete draws his gun, pointing it upward as he moves onward. Out from the burial structure comes a loud roar! Pete fires a few rounds and I run into the darkness for cover, trying not to pee my pants.

Pete is crouched on the ground, hoping to dodge any shots that may come from the inside the stone building. No more shots are made, but a voice loudly emerges from the foyer that we recognize. I shine the flashlight at the edifice again and we see Sergeant José Lujan, visibly shaking, frantically explaining he was playing a practical joke. — Haha. Not very funny for Pete and I. By the grace of God we're all okay.

José had entered from the back of the cemetery and had poorly planned a practical joke on whoever was assigned to the call. We just happened to be his unfortunate victims. We all survived two rounds of friendly fire that missed their marks.

Spare Tire Puzzle

Shortly after the mausoleum adventure, during the same year of 1988, came one of the worst snowstorms ever to hit Aldea Baca. It's late night and word comes in that an elderly lady is stuck in deep snow with a flat tire. Two officers arrive at the location. After struggling with the car jack for a half hour, they radio in, requesting more help because the snow is so deep. They could not get the car lifted high enough to make room to remove the tire. Most in northern Arizona don't deal well with white fluffy stuff falling out of the sky. A quarter inch of it and schools and businesses close.

I get called in to assist. Icy roads make the drive time longer than usual. When I arrive and park behind the other squad car, I notice that the officers were able to get the tire off, but they were not able to get the spare tire on. I go over to try my luck.

I'm struggling to put the tire on the rim. Lifting it a number of times, trying to line up the lug holes with the bolts in the wheel assembly. Lifting, turning, pushing. Lifting, turning, pushing. Huffing, puffing. The tire has to be the right size. It came from the car's trunk.

It's late and cold for the shivering old lady. Officer Franco tells me that he'll give her a ride home. She really didn't want to drive in the snow all the way from Aldea Baca to her home in the outskirts. The lady is so appreciative she gives Franco and me a big hug. She thanks all the officers for all their help. Then she looks at me on my knees holding the tire, and says, "You know, you've been trying to get the tire on backwards. Turn it around and it should slide on easily."

Duhhhhh! Forty minutes I was fumbling with this. I didn't know the front of the tire versus the back. None of the officers noticed either. Five minutes later, I had the tire on securely.

We decide to park the lady's car in a private lot and lock it up safely. She was so sweet, giving me another big hug in appreciation. The old lady will safely get to her warm home in Officer Franco's squad car.

Vested Interest

I don't hesitate to say that being married now with my college sweetheart, Tessie, is wonderful. Now that I am a seasoned policeman, I'm experiencing what it is to be a rookie husband. I'm learning. Part of this new lifestyle is finding how to balance time at work and time with my wife. Because I'm still working night shifts, we value whatever hours we can be together, especially on weekends. We may make plans, but realize that they can always change due to the unpredictable circumstances associated with a policeman's life.

The weather forecast for the coming weekend looks excellent so my wife pencils in a date for Saturday. I can tell by her face expression that she's cooking up something special. The image of her smile stays in my head while I drive to work.

After an hour patrolling the streets, I get a call for assistance. When I arrive at the scene, an officer is trying to wrestle a handgun away from a lady in front of her home. In the course of the struggle, a number of rounds are being shot. She's not very big but, nevertheless, adrenaline is running and she's giving him a run for his money. I learn that she is so angry with her husband that she's attempting to settle matters with a gun. She's not intentionally shooting at the police. The officer had entered the house earlier and somehow managed to get her away from the husband and moved her outside.

So, when I arrive, he's having trouble trying to control her and the gun. I join in the scuffle as she's pulling off rounds and hysterically trying to get back to confront her husband. When she turns her attention at my presence, the other officer is able to get her arms behind her back into a solid hold. After he takes control of the pistol, we eventually get her booked for reckless discharge of a weapon in the city limits and domestic violence. Seems the finale of a good day's work.

My shift ends at 11:00pm, but I don't get home until 12:30am. Tessie is awake in the livingroom waiting for me because it is Friday . . . turned Saturday. Her being up means she wants talk about what we will do together today. We don't get too many of weekends off. As we are talking about what to do, I go into the back room of our home to get into pajamas. I take off my shirt and remove my vest. I take off my Sam Brown—the belt that carries all the police equipment required for duty.

We usually don't discuss my work day, but Tessie asks, "Braden, did you have a tough day? How did you get shot?"

I tell her that I didn't, but she just makes a face that indicates I'm mistaken.

She quips, "I don't know very much about bullets, but it sure looks like there are two bullet holes in your vest. When did you get shot?"

I inspect my vest and, sure enough, there are two rounds in it. I look at her and start feeling around my chest to see if I was hurt. I take off my undershirt to be sure there's no bleeding.

"I am telling you, I didn't know that I got shot."

She says, "Well, you gotta tell somebody at the office and formally report it."

I let her know that I have to get dressed and go back to work for a while. Damn paperwork.

She reminds me, "We're getting up early, so you hurry up. Do whatever you need to do, but I want us to go to Flagstaff."

I hurry back to the office 'cause I know protocol: Of course, if one gets shot, you have to file a report! I have to explain how it happened, and if I discharged my weapon. Also, the vest is no longer good. It has to be replaced. When I get to the office, I inform the sergeant that I got shot in the chest. He looked at me with a questioning expression.

"My wife found holes in the vest."

I open up my shirt and show him where flattened lead chunks are still stuck in the vest.

The sargeant starts laughing, knowing that it will take me two hours just to fill out report forms. After I finished the arrest report, I immediately start working on an addendum—a report on the damaged vest—and cross-reference both with the case number. Now it's about 3:10am. I decline to go to the emergency room for a checkup. Sarge waves me off. By the time I get in the house, it's 3:30. I climb into the bed as quietly as possible, then wait 'till about 7:00. Tessie shakes me into semi-consciousness. I stumble into some clothes and tell my numb body that it's in for a fun day driving, walking, shopping, eating, and enjoying the free time with my dear wife.

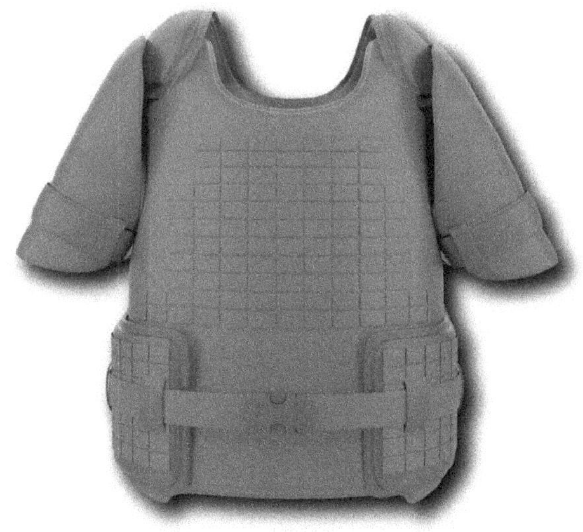

Above: Illustration 131565709 © Nerthuz | Dreamstime.com

Dispatching the Dispatcher

In general, police work consists of many hours of boredom, interspersed by bursts of terrifying activity. As captain, I often have much tedious paperwork to do at the office. At the same time, I have to keep tabs on other employees and make sure we function as well as possible as a department.

There are usually nine or twelve patrol officers working a shift. Today, I notice that, among each of the officers assigned to one of the twelve city districts, one guy who is assigned to a northern district was getting calls to a southern district. During rush-hour traffic, that's a good twenty minute drive. Having officers in one district being sent across town is a waste of time and is not an efficient way to assist the public in a timely manner.

The dispatching seems illogical to me. I must check to see what is going on and if there is a way to improve the assignments. I use our secure radio channel to call the supervisor. She says, "Well, I have a new dispatcher here and she's doing the best she can."

In a vocal tone that captures my frustration, I say, "Okay. I would like to try to straighten it out and see if we can get dispatching to be more practical for the officers. Maybe I can come in and take a look and see why we're scattered all over the city?"

"Fine," says the supervisor. "Come to the dispatch center now. I'll help you look over what's in place and see where we can improve."

I arrive and make a discovery. From the time a notification arrives indicating something is wrong and potentially very dangerous, it takes about twenty or more minutes for an officer to arrive at the designated location. According to the supervisor, it can taken even longer. Heck, a burglar would have enough time to truck out the contents of a house!

The next clear step is to meet the dispatcher who is assigned to sending out the officers on calls. When we meet, I swear she looks about twelve years old, but probably is in her late teens. The dispatch supervisor saw me interacting with the young lady, so she comes over to listen in on our conversation.

I point to a city map and ask the dispatcher, "You know this officer here? In what district is this officer? Where is he supposed to be?"

She puts her finger where the officer is based in a northern district.

I ask, "Well, why did you send him from there all the way down to a southern district?"

The young lady tells me, "It isn't far for them to drive. I just look on the map to see where they need to go."

As she's explaining this to me, she indicating the distance on the map by holding her thumb and fore-finger a half inch apart. She has no clue how many miles that gap between her fingers really represents. I had the urge to show her another finger gesture, but refrained, tightly grinding my teeth.

I look at one officer's route, then another officer's route, and another. The supervisor must have noticed the heat raising up my neck and nudges me out of the dispatching room. The incompetence was too much for me too handle with any composure. I thank her for leading me to calmer grounds. I didn't want to blow my stack in the office.

The supervisor finally confesses, "I'll let you know something. I was a little leery when we hired her. She previously worked at a movie theater and was let go. The reason given was that she kept running head first into the plexiglass door of a popcorn machine. The final time, she actually broke the door off by the hinges."

"Oh geez," I quip, "No wonder why she can't grasp the logistics for dispatching. We urgently need to make some changes here."

I look at the supervisor and say with a grin, "Today, I've come this close (holdup my thumb and forefinger a half-inch apart), to walking off the job."

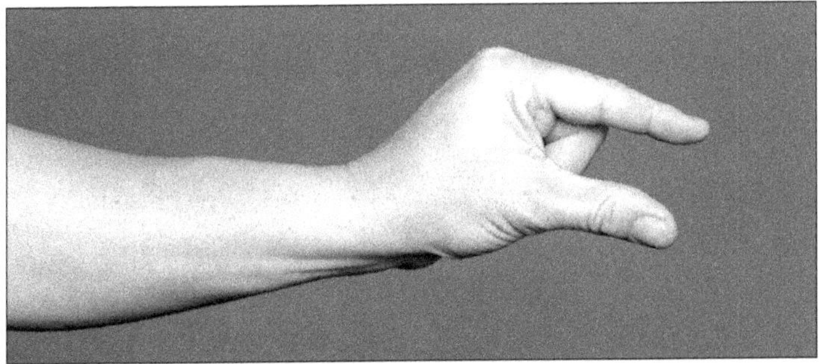

Toe or Tongue Tag?

It is a typical summertime. A late evening that retains the heat of the day. Only a decade before this year of 1975, in-home air conditioning was rare. Even now, not everybody has it. If they do, it's just a small conditioner in one room that hangs outside the window.

My regular work today is interrupted with a call to a home disturbance. The caller said that there is a lady screaming for help at her home on Silver Fox Lane. I arrive ten minutes after receiving the call to find four or five neighbors standing in front of the home, which looks familiar. They tell me that there's a woman inside yelling for help. Her voice carries a distance because many of her windows are open this hot evening. I can't clearly tell if the lady is on the first or second floor.

I go to the front door. It's locked, so I quickly search for a key that may be hiding under the front door matt, under a flower pot, and above the door frame. No luck. I walk to check the back door and find it also locked. From the back of the home, I can clearly hear the woman screaming.

I gotta get in the house, so I decide to break the into the front door. Without special equipment, I kick in the door and go in. It's pitch black inside. I can hear the woman screaming near the end of the hall. I'm guessing she's in a bathroom. From burglaries and other calls for service in this neighborhood, I've learned that the layout of homes in this area are traditionally built with three or four doorways in the hall leading into bedrooms. I pull the gun from my holster and start cautiously walking though the front room toward the hallway. Out of the corner of my eye I see movement to my left. I pivot quickly and fire twice, hitting the image dead center only to realize it was my own reflection in a tall floor mirror.

After my gun shots, I hear screeching behind me, alerting me that about a half a dozen neighbors had followed me into the house. I move forward and clear the next room and then the third room. Obviously they were three bedrooms, so I get to the end of the hall. A woman's voice is coming from a behind the door. A line of light marks the threshold. She repeatedly screams, "Help me! Help me!"

I approach close to the door to announce, "I'm the police. Is there someone in there with you?"

Somewhat hysterical, she only responds with "Help me! Help me!"

I attempt to open the door, but it's locked. Many bathroom doors in homes have a lock and often owners just leave a key atop the door's trim. I check, but feel nothing. So, I lean against it with my weight of 220 pounds and the door gives way.

Behold, in front of my eyes is a naked lady laying in the tub with no water in it.

Trying to only look at her face, I ask what's wrong and she directs me to her foot. I look and see her left big toe is stuck in the faucet. It's an antique looking faucet that she had put in to replace old hardware. She got the toe up the spigot and couldn't get it out. She even let the water out of the tub, thinking it may somehow set the appendage free.

As I listen to her story, my brain doesn't register that she's naked. I'm focused on how to liberate her toe. Then I become fully aware that half a dozen people nosed their way into the bathroom all concerned about their neighbor. Now the lady is embarrassed and crying. My plea for her to calm down doesn't have any effect. A thoughtful neighbor hands me a bath towel to cover her private parts.

I try to wiggle the toe free and fail. I ask if there is anything in the kitchen to lubricate the toe, such as butter or Crisco oil. One guy suggests WD-40. The toe is stuck in there pretty good. We tried a few lubricants without success. A possible solution is to call the fire department. They have all the tools for such home emergencies.

It doesn't take the firemen long to figure out what to do. After fully ensuring the woman that she wouldn't be harmed, they get an electric saw and cut the faucet off close to the wall. They get her semi-dressed and head for the hospital. She's safely in good hands. I am glad the case is over and that I don't have to worry any longer. A fireman reminds me why her house looked familiar. She is well-known in town, actively serving on various community boards.

About a year later, I get served a subpoena. Along with the police department, I am now being sued by the ungrateful lady for breaking down the front door, shooting the mirror, opening the bathroom door without a key, and destruction of the faucet. When my wife hears of this, she states matter of factly that "no good deed goes unpunished."

Not a Peace Pipe

"Gun shots being fired." The address where the gunshots were coming from is given directly to me. Usually only one officer is dispatched to a call like this. When you get to the scene and it looks like you need help, a second or a third person may be sent. So, I get dispatched out the door by myself.

Within ten minutes I arrive at the location. There's a house that obviously has just one light turned on. It's deadly quiet, but I see what looks like shadows moving in the house. I decided it's best not to rush in. It's better to be careful and patiently wait a few minutes in case somebody runs out of the house toward me or ambush me if I try walking in.

I wait. One minute. Two minutes. Three minutes under these circumstances seems like an hour, so I start walking to the front entrance. Just as I get to the door, my eyes are draw to movement above my head. Somebody leaps down from the home's roof, lands behind me, and strikes me across my lower back with a heavy metal pipe. Contacting some vertebrae, it was painful.

Turning around, I hit the guy on the jaw. Out cold, he lands on his back. I turn him over and immediately cuff him. Another guy on the roof saw what happened and scampers away not to be seen again.

There's at least one more guy in the house. I yell in for him to come out. He comes out alright, swinging a baseball bat at me. Fortunately, I noticed it, ducked and simultaneously threw a punch to his stomach—just above the bladder area. That strike opened some flood gates: buckling foreward, he immediately shit in his pants. I have an extra set of plastic cuffs and put them on him. I finish up the evening at the station in usual fashion.

While waiting a few minutes in the landing area for the elevator to escort my two handcuffed friends to the second floor jail, a brand new officer sees me. It was only his second or third day on the job. When I return to the first floor, I see him in the same spot, looking somewhat paralyzed. I ask how he's doing.

He tells me he noticed that my shirt is torn off my back, exposing welts, and that I looked lucky to survive a beating. Even the night shift officer in charge told me I couldn't book the men because I was out of uniform. The rookie is a relatively small statured fella and I am not. Could he withstand the beating I took tonight? The poor chap was doubting the decision in choosing police work for a career. We talked a while. He plans to talk it over with his girlfriend.

I head home and go straight to bed to enjoy a few solid hours of a peaceful, dreamless sleep.

The next day, I receive a call from Yolanda, who transported the two men to the magistrate's office. She reports that the first man to appear in court submits to protocol without a fuss. The second man also appeared in court, wearing fresh clothes provided by the city.

Standing in front of the bench, he tells the judge, "Your honor, I plead guilty. I don't ever wanna see Officer Vicentin again. Although I tried to hit him with a bat, he hit me so hard that I don't think I could survive another punch like that." The judge told him that he couldn't plead guilty because he was only being formally charged for now.

I don't know the outcome of these cases. I was never called and never got a summons. I suspect the two men were let go.

Getting Fired Up

I am assigned to a State, Alcohol Beverage and Tobacco officer—an ATF man who is working in plain clothes, driving an unmarked car. I, on the other hand, am in full uniform and riding a marked unit from the City of Aldea Baca. I'm driving behind him heading to a bar called El Abrevadero Feliz on West El Paso Drive. During the day, it is a known hotspot where young people congregate. Many are 70s-type free spirits, while a good number are simply lost souls—two common qualities among young folk in most cities. The bar has a shady history. We've been called to this location often for one reason or another.

The ATF had gotten word that there were guns being sold illegally out of the back door, some weapons no doubt had trickled in from Vietnam vets. The ATF officer gives me a briefing, mentioning that there is a confidential informant inside the bar that is in regular communication with ATF. Our orders are to try to work our way to the management and learn what is going on. We are prepared to approach the bar in a way suitable for apprehending armed criminals.

The Abrevadero Feliz is on a busy street with two lanes in both directions, separated by a median. I follow the ATF man's car into a crossover lane where we wait for traffic to pass so we can drive directly into the bar's parking area. I'm looking ahead, anticipating what we'll find inside.

In a compressed second, my car is hit by a speeding vehicle, pushing it into the AFT officer's car, and flames burst out at the front and side. His tank must have ruptured with sparks igniting the gasoline. I can't get out my door because most of the driver's side was crumpled into an interlocking garble of metal. I look for another way out. The only solution is to break a window. I see flames outside the driver's side, so I look to the passenger's side window. I'm a pretty big guy, I didn't think I could fit through. I should be able to get through the larger back window. I realize that the thick, steel mesh barrier cage installed to protect officers from prisoners placed in the back seat is missing. The force of the car accident drove the spare tire through the back seat, knocking the barrier loose. I grab the shotgun that is standard equipment in the car, blow out the window, and flee the burning car. I quickly move toward the car that hit us and get the driver out to safety.

I look back at the crash site. The ATF officer is okay. Seeing the collision, a thoughtful trucker was using his own extinguisher, spraying the flames into submission. With stinging in my back, I manage to walk over to the trucker, thanking him for his help. He deserves much credit. Without spraying down the cars, I'm not so sure I would've been able to get the driver out of the vehicle that hit us on the roadway.

We're standing on the shoulder of the road, four lanes across from the El Abrevadero Feliz. Two fire trucks arrive and they clear the area of bystanders. Six or more firemen are trying to put out the remaining areas still burning around the cars. Out of a relative calmness, I now hear bullets firing! The stock of rounds in the squad car are being set off from the heat of the fire. Stray bullets can ricochet in any direction and I worry about the firemen and others. The firemen don't stop, set on getting the fires totally out.

The ATF guy is sitting on the curb. Somewhat dazed, I walk over to him, saying I'm sorry for what happened, my car hitting his and all. I'm glad that he seems to be relatively okay. I don't feel well at all and just want to get to bed and passout. Although I can barely function, I choose not to go to the hospital to be checked out. Other officers fill out all the paperwork . . . thank God. A fellow officer gives me a ride home. It's 7:00am. Tessie is ready to go to work. Upon sight of me, she panics some, but I assure her that I'm fine.

I sleep for three or four hours. When I wake up, my mind is buzzing with all the factors of the crash. I force myself to get to the station and double-check the paperwork. I believe it looks fine, but I am distracted by intensifying pains. I decide to go to the hospital. Perhaps the doc can give me something to alleviate the main areas of discomfort. After a careful study of X-rays, the doctor tells me that I have a vertebre with a hairline crack. Because of my youth and strength, he thinks I'll be fine . . . for now. "You'll probably need to get the spine checked again in twenty or thirty years. In later age, you're gonna need a cane. The crack usually brings on an arthritic condition, placing great pressure on the vertebrae. With the gradual disintegration, an operation may help make daily activities bearable."

It is easier to be positive on some days than other days.

Solitary Confinement

After her husband passed three years ago, Grandma Teresa—known affectionately as Abuela Teresa—has been living alone. Her children and grandchildren live about five hours away, but she hasn't seen them in a decade. They sometimes call on holidays or for her birthday, if they remember. For the past year, Teresa has been essentially bedridden. As an Aldea Baca local, police officers know her and regularly stop by for a wellness check.

I got to know Teresa's history, family background, her old hobbies, jobs . . . And, she got to know me too. We are friends. So, it is not a total surprise that she calls me at work today.

I pickup the phone on my desk. "Aldea Baca Police Department. This is Officer Vicentin. How may I help you?"

Teresa responds, saying, "Buenos dias Braden . . . I mean Officer Vicentin. I just wondered if you had some time to stop by for a few minutes for a visit?"

I can guess that she's just feeling lonely and wants some company, to feel in touch with the real world.

"Sure Teresa. I can stop by in about thirty minutes, Okay?"

When I arrive, I knock on her door and announce "Teresa! Braden here! Can I come in?"

The door isn't locked. Knowing she's expecting me, I enter her living room and can see through an archway into the kitchen where she's standing with a walker at the kitchen sink.

"What are you doing up on your feet Teresa? I hope you're being careful. The vapor trails from your teapot bring a nice aroma!"

I help her get seated at the kitchen table and pour us cups of Lipton tea. One teaspoon of sugar for my cup and three for hers as usual. A plate of assorted cookies have been set out. I think to myself of the tremendous effort this fragile, rawboned granny made just for my visit.

As has become a tradition, she asks me to read a few pages from a book. Whatever book is nearby when I show up, that's what I read. The closest at hand is titled *The Monkey Wrench Gang* by Edward Abbey. I read for about five minutes from Chapter 1 and then ask, "Teresa, do you ever finish reading the books I read to you?"

She says, "No. . . I just like to hear somebody's voice." Then we talk for almost a half hour, sharing a melody of sentences that are nearly void of content but connect our existence. When I'm about to exit the door to return to my duties, I look back to see a fatigued Teresa at rest in a rocking chair, appearing somewhat angelic.

A week passes and our dispatcher receives word from Teresa's neighbor. The visitor relates how she just arrived at Teresa's home to bring her a homemade green chili chicken stew. She finds her very very ill. The dispatcher radios my squad car with a directive: "Officer Vicentin, Teresa, the lady you visit on Upper Mesa Road, is quite ill. Can you go to check on her?"

I call for an ambulance. We arrive at the home at the same time. The EMT's realize they can do nothing. Abuela Teresa's last syllable is muffled as her last breath disperses.

Foiled Again

There's a railroad crossing at Delano Avenue and East Navajo. It seems like every night between midnight and five in the morning the lights there start flashing for no reason at all. I'm puzzled. No train. Just flashing lights. I'm out in the wee hours patrolling, and sure enough, intermittent bursts of red lights start signaling.

One night I'm inspired to get out and walk along the track. Why? Well, a story my mom told me when I was very young came to mind. She told me that during her youth, kids would put metal rods on the rails and somehow short circuit the electrical system. This may be fun activity for the mischievous, but a potentially dangerous game to play.

I park on the street close to the tracks and start to walk, inspecting the rails and any electrical boxes and lines. It's quiet with just moonlight as a companion, until I notice a human figure far ahead laying between the tracks.

When get closer, I can make out that a dishevelled man is lying on his back between the tracks. In contrast to his grubby worn torn clothing are gleaming bits of aluminum foil over his hands and head.

As I approach, I ask, "Hey buddy, how are you? Everything okay?"

He sits up waving at me, saying "Hi officer." Sure, I'm fine."

"Good. I'm glad you're okay this fine evening." Staring at his self-made silver beanie, my curiosity spurs on some questioning.

"Does your hat keep your head warm enough these nights?"

In a most lucid fashion, he explains, "Oh, the hat is to protect my brain from the sun's magnetic rays."

"But it's night," I point out. "Isn't the hat better to wear during the daytime?"

"Seems best to keep it on all the time. I want to be as safe as possible."

And I have to jump to the next items of wear. "How about the aluminum gloves?"

Wide eyed, he quickly responds. "Oh, they protect me from the aliens!"

I carry on a conversation with the man and eventually say, "Well, the hat and gloves may be good shields, but we can get you excellent protection tonight if you sleep where I work. You know I'm gonna have to take you in to the police station."

"Oh no," he says with a plea. "You can't do that."

"Why not? Why not? We only want to help you to have a comfortable night."

He responds logically. "Because they will take my helmet away and never give it back to me! They never give it back! I won't go there ever again."

I eventually persuade him to come to the station, telling the other officers that I solved the mystery of the flashing railroad crossing lights. While laying in the middle of the tracks, the man would stretch out his arms. Both of his hands, covered with aluminum foil, would touch the rails and inadvertently short circuit the lighting system.

I wasn't the only officer in the department who dealt with the homeless at one time or another. There are no shelters for them to find solace. Hopefully there will be in the future.

I never saw this gentle man again. Is he okay? Did any humans or aliens offer him shelter?

Female Fists

There's a fancy restaurant in downtown Aldea Baca called the Duke and Duchess Lounge. It's located catty-corner to the old courthouse building on Jefferson Street. It's certainly a wonderful place for anyone to have a scrumptious dinner and enjoy the cozy Victorian atmosphere. As anyone could guess, a cadre of political types regularly frequent the establishment.

There is rarely any serious trouble at The Duke. As their usual meeting place, the politicians are very guarded whenever there, wishing not to create any problems. However, this Friday evening I get a call to investigate a disturbance.

The restaurant is only two minutes from the police station. I park at the front door. Entering the lounge, I see two semiconscious male patrons, sprawled on the floor next to bar stools. To my surprise, there are two gorgeous, athletic women standing over them in triumphal poses. Their svelte figures no doubt belie their martial skills.

Strolling up to the ladies, I simply want to ask what's going on. Before I finish the question, I realize that somehow I had been thrown out the door onto the street! I don't even know how that happened to me—a six foot two, 220 pound lawman. I rise off the pavement and I go back

into the lounge prepared to use some force if necessary.

The ladies are now in a booth, sitting next to a senator whom I recognize. Perhaps his companions are his hired bodyguards? The women see me approaching and start to come toward me like two Pit Bulls. Then the senator intervenes, giving permission to let me visit with him.

I know the debonair senator. He knows that I know of his shady doings, kickbacks and all. I put that knowledge to the side to focus on the present situation. Yes, the ladies are his bodyguards. They supposedly were protecting the senator from the two men.

After talking with the bartender and a few others, all I could do is ask the senator and company to leave the restaurant. They immediately protest. I hint that if they do decide to stay, their names will likely be given to the press.

Sheepishly, the government man and the Pit Bulls depart the premises without further disturbance.

Signaling for Help

In the office, I could overhear the sergeant and dispatcher trying to contact unit 35, the car number of an officer out on patrol. They have his last known address where he was assigned to in the district, up on unpaved Old Mesa Road.

A short time later, while I'm out on patrol, I receive a call from the dispatcher. There has been no response from car 35. I need to go out on a manhunt. I cross districts in search of the missing officer and squad car, covering the main roads and side streets one by one.

When I make a turn off of Old Mesa Road, I spot car 35. The lights are on. The engine is running. Oddly, I don't see an officer around. I radio in that "the car was located; going out to inspect."

As I exit my car, there's a pervasive smell of fresh gunpowder. Cautiously approaching car 35, flashlight in hand, I see an empty seat behind the wheel. Then, I hear screaming.

"Get me out of here! Get me out of here! I'm stuck!"

From what direction was his voice coming from? I look around, but don't see him.

"Where the hell are you!?"

In a breathy voice of exasperation, he says "I'm on the passenger side." I recognize that it's the voice of fellow officer Lance Bowman.

My flashlight beam illuminates the back of a dark blue uniform. He's curled up in a ball and I can't see his face. So I go around to the front of the car to try to get on the other side. I can't walk to the side door because that side of the car is at the edge of a cliff.

On the passenger side, just above the window, there's a gapping hole through the roof. I have to ask. "How'd this hole get here Lance?"

"I wanted to open the passenger side window without getting out of the car," he says. "So I slid over and started to roll down the window. Somehow my coat got wedged between the door in the shotgun rack. I couldn't get to the radio."

Pinned with his face against the door, he further explains, "Well, to get help, all I could think of is try to signal someone. I was able to extend my finger just far enough to hit the shotgun trigger. It shot and a bunch of shit fell all over me from the roof."

I try to open the driver side door, find it locked, and use a *slim jim* to get it open. Pieces of white roof insulation are everywhere. Now, while I'm laughing uncontrollably at this comic scene, the sergeant arrives.

Regaining most of my composure, I explain the situation to the sergeant. We can't get Lance out through the passenger door without the possibility of him falling down into the ravine. So, I drive the car forward to safer ground, cut his coat sleeve free, and pull him out. He's covered head to waist in insulation flakes, looking like Frosty the Snowman.

I receive the honor of writing up the report.

Working the Magic

Sergeant Allard calls in, speaking in a skittish voice. "Captain Vicentin, we have a problem. Patrolman Fernandez pulled over a guy on Mission Street and arrested him for about a half a pound of marijuana. He's a Navajo named Oliver Bilid."

"That's a felony charge," I note. "So, what's the problem?"

Allard says in a staccato fashion, "Well, of course we booked the man and he's in a cell now. I accepted the evidence and approved the report. Just as I finished the paperwork, Officer Lopez was going to place the bag of marijuana in the evidence room for me. Glancing at the bag, his unibrow furrowed with a curious expression. He opened it up under his nose and inhaled deeply. Then he gave me a frozen, blank stare. He raised his hands upwards and told me 'It's only tobacco!' Lopez even pointed out that the name of the tobacco company was on the bag. — What should I do!?"

I emphasize, "You write down exactly what you did and that you notified me. I'll take care of it from here."

Allard asks sheepishly, "You want me to shade the text anywhere?"

"No!" I exclaim. "Let's not worry about that now. You caught the mistake after the fact. We'll go ahead and deal with repercussions later."

"Are we gonna be in big trouble because of this?" he asks.

"Probably" is my single word reply.

He follows with "Am I gonna be in big trouble?"

"Probably," reinforced with another "Probably."

Allard is a relatively new sergeant, so I give him clear instructions. "In order to begin our clean up of this mess, we first gotta get Mr. Bilid out of jail. Afterwards, get the paperwork and bring it to me."

We bypass the usual thousand dollar bail for a felony. No bail.

"Allard, tell me we didn't impound the car."

"Sorry sir. We did sir. But my cousin works at the lot and I'm sure we can get the car out without any cost to Mr. Bilid and we won't get billed either."

"Great," I add. "That's at least one hurdle we can get over.

Sergeant Allard's next duty is to get Bilid out of jail. Bilid's feathers are ruffled. He doesn't speak out, but certainly looks somewhat upset. I realize there may be a way to give Bilid an attitude adjustment. I call in Officer McDoogal, who is one lousy patrolman, but one who is blessed with a jovial character that is contagious. His duty now is to take Mr. Bilid out for a nice dinner, including an open tab for beverages of their choice.

"But I'm on duty and still in uniform!" snaps McDoogal.

I think for a few minutes and suggest "Well, how about I put you on administrative leave and you switch from your uniform in to civilian clothing?"

"Okay," McDoogal says with a smile. He seems happy with the assignment and they head off to Bar Herradura on Washington Street. They stay even after closing time, being the last to leave the premises.

A month later Mr. Bilid is called in to attend a risk management meeting. Hopefully all paperwork can be done and we can close this case. We're anxious with the possibility that Bilid may bring up accusations about being arrested under false claims and his car being impounded.

Sergeant Allard stands nervously at attention. His forehead has beaded up with sweat. The armpits of his light blue long-sleeved shirt have turned as dark blue as his tie from perspiration. We'll soon find out how much trouble we're in.

Mr. Bilid somberly enters the room and asks to make a statement.

Bilid's demeanor brightens. "Oh, I'm happy that the officers proved I didn't have marijuana. They took me out for dinner with drinks and drove me home. My car was returned. The officers were all very polite and professional."

Without hesitating, Bilid signed all the papers.

Shrugging their shoulders, the people in charge of the legal department close the folder on the case and we depart the room with some sighs of relief.

Officer McDoogal had worked his magic perfectly.

Rooftop Jogging

Since the early 1970s, Aldea Baca has been experiencing a number of burglaries in the downtown area. Most of the buildings in this historical district have flat roofs, a traditional style common in Arizona. As "all streets lead to Rome," in Aldea Baca they lead to the central plaza, a highlight for locals and visitors who can enjoy the trees' shade while being entertained watching passersby. The business owners and others can't figure out how thieves are breaking into their shops. Are they entering in from the roofs? Do they somehow enter a store and hideout inside a building's crawlspace between the roof and the building itself, waiting until after hours to grab the goods and escape?

Along with the police department's input, the shopkeepers and others decide that we organize a stake out in the area to see what we can discover. Over the next few weeks, a number of officers take turns stealthy observing the commercial buildings located in the historic district.

As predictable, today I'm ordained for the duty. I suit up and drive my squad car behind a store about four blocks from the plaza. There are two ways to get on the rooftops. One is to go into an establishment and use their interior stairway. Another way is to climb up one of the fire escapes located on the outside of the buildings, usually on a side street or behind the building. Scaling up a fire escape ladder is a mini gym workout in itself,

so we prefer using the stairs.

After exchanging pleasantries with a shop owner before he closes the store for the night, I head to the rooftop. Next to the doorway exit, there's a giant swamp cooler. I stand sentinel against it since it offers a good position for observing the surroundings while being concealed in its shadow cast from the setting sun. Two hours go by and I'm feeling the cool of the night. The home lights start to flicker off as the folks of Aldea Baca turn in and the town eventually sleeps.

Another couple hours go by. The air has cooled since sundown. The chill is keeping me awake. It's a clear night, perfect for stargazing and quietly scanning the roof tops. Across the street, under the spell of silence, a shadow rises. I discern a guy's head and shoulders pop up above a roof. He's no doubt a spotter, looking along the rooftops to be sure nobody else could see him or his accomplice entering the scene. He disappears a second and then reappears, pulling himself onto the roof.

I rush downstairs to get across the street and onto the roof of another store. I try to be as quiet as possible and work my way closer to the scout. Just ten feet behind him, an old roof board cracks loudly under my foot that bears my full weight of 220 pounds. The lookout man